MEET OFFICER Jerry

Greg Moskal

Rosen REAL READERS

Rosen Classroom Books and Materials

Officer Jerry is a policeman. The police keep people **safe** and stop **crime**.

Officer Jerry's helper is a dog named Bruno. Officer Jerry **trains** Bruno to do police work.

Officer Jerry and Bruno ride around town to make sure everyone is safe.

Bruno helps Officer Jerry search buildings for people who break the law.

Bruno helps Jerry fight crime by finding things that can hurt people. Bruno uses his sense of smell to find **drugs**.

Another police officer calls Officer Jerry on his police radio. She tells Officer Jerry to check out a possible break-in.

Officer Jerry drives to the store and tells Bruno to check it out. Bruno jumps out of the car and runs into the store.

Officer Jerry looks around the store too. No one is inside and everything is safe.

Officer Jerry also takes Bruno to schools to talk to children. He and Bruno show the children how they work as a **team**.

Officer Jerry tells the children to **obey** the law and say no to drugs.

GLOSSARY

crime An act that is against the law.

drug Something a person can take to change the way she thinks, feels, or acts.

obey To do what someone else asks you to do, or to follow the rules.

safe To be free from danger.

team A group of people who work or play together.

train Teaching someone to do something the right way.